THiS BOOK BELONGS TO

I celebrated World Book Day 2018
with this brilliant gift from my local
bookseller, Macmillan Children's Books,
Andy Griffiths and Terry Denton.

CELEBRATE STORIES. LOVE READING.

This book has been specially written and published to celebrate **World Book Day**. We are a charity that offers every child and young person the opportunity to read and love books by offering you the chance to have a book of your own. To find out more – as well as oodles of fun activities and reading recommendations to continue your reading journey, visit **worldbookday.com**

World Book Day in the UK and Ireland is made possible by generous sponsorship from National Book Tokens, participating publishers, booksellers, authors and illustrators. The £1* book tokens are a gift from your local bookseller.

World Book Day works in partnership with a number of charities, all of which are working to encourage a love of reading for pleasure.

The National Literacy Trust is an independent charity that encourages children to enjoy reading. Just ten minutes of reading every day can make a big difference to how well you do at school and to how successful you could be in life. **literacytrust.org.uk**

The Reading Agency inspires people of all ages and backgrounds to read for pleasure and empowerment. It runs the Summer Reading Challenge in partnership with libraries, as well as supporting reading groups in schools and libraries all year round. Find out more and join your local library. **summerreadingchallenge.org.uk**

World Book Day also facilitates fundraising for:

Book Aid International, an international book donation and library development charity. Every year, it provides one million books to libraries and schools in communities where children would otherwise have little or no opportunity to read. **bookaid.org.uk**

Read for Good, which motivates children in schools to read for fun through its sponsored read that thousands of schools run on World Book Day and throughout the year. The money raised provides new books and resident storytellers in all the UK's children's hospitals. **readforgood.org**

*€1.50 in Ireland

Andy Griffiths lives in an amazing treehouse with his friend Terry and together they make funny books, just like the one you're holding in your hands right now. Andy writes the words and Terry draws the pictures. If you'd like to know more, read this book (or visit www.andygriffiths.com.au).

Terry Denton lives in an amazing treehouse with his friend Andy and together they make funny books, just like the one you're holding in your hands right now. Terry draws the pictures and Andy writes the words. If you'd like to know more, read this book (or visit www.terrydenton.com).

Books by Andy Griffiths and Terry Denton

Coming soon!

ANDY GRIFFITHS & TERRY DENTON

A TREEHOUSE ADVENTURE

TERRY'S DUMB DOT STORY

MACMILLAN CHILDREN'S BOOKS

First published 2018 in Pan by Pan Macmillan Australia Pty Ltd

First published in the UK 2018 by Macmillan Children's Books
an imprint of Pan Macmillan
20 New Wharf Road, London N1 9RR
Associated companies throughout the world
www.panmacmillan.com

ISBN 978-1-5098-8122-2

Pan Macmillan does not have any control over, or any responsibility for,
any author or third-party websites referred to in or on this book.

1 3 5 7 9 8 6 4 2

A CIP catalogue record for this book is available from the British Library.

Typeset in 14/18 Minion Pro by Seymour Designs
Printed and bound by CPI Group (UK) Ltd, Croydon CR0 4YY

A TREEHOUSE ADVENTURE

TERRY'S DUMB DOT STORY

Hi, my name is Andy.

This is my friend Terry.

pencil

Terry →

We live in the world's most amazing treehouse.

It's got a bowling alley,

a tank full of man-eating sharks,

a chocolate waterfall,

the world's scariest rollercoaster,

7

a pet-grooming salon (run by our neighbour, Jill),

a secret underground laboratory,

and a whole bunch of other really cool stuff that I haven't got time to tell you about now because our publisher, Mr Big Nose, is in a big hurry for this book and if we don't finish it in time he will get so angry that his nose will explode.

THE DAY MR. BIGNOSE GOT SO ANGRY HIS NOSE EXPLODED.

You see, as well as being our home, the treehouse is also where we make books together. I write the words and Terry draws the pictures.

'It's not fair,' says Terry. 'How come *you* always get to tell the story?'

'Because *I'm* the narrator,' I say. 'And *you're* the illustrator.'

'I can narrate *too*, you know,' says Terry.
  'No, you can't,' I say.
  'Yes, I can!' says Terry.

'CAN'T!'

 'CAN!'

'CAN'T!'

 'CAN!'

'CAN'T!'

 'CAN!'

I'm just about to yell 'CAN'T' even bigger when Jill comes along.

'What are you two arguing about now?' she says.

'Terry says he *can* narrate and I say he

CAN'T!'

13

'There's a better way to settle this than by shouting at each other,' says Jill.

'*Really?*' I say. 'How?'

'Let Terry do some narration and see how it goes,' says Jill.

'But he's an illustrator! Illustrators can't narrate—*everybody* knows that!'

'That's not true,' says Jill. 'What about Dr Moose? He wrote *and* illustrated *The Splat in the Hat*.'

'And Boris Bentback wrote and illustrated *Where the Filed Things Are*, one of the most famous and best-loved children's books about office management ever!'

'And who could forget Beatnik Potty?' says Jill. 'I *love* her animal stories!'

Jill has a point, I guess. 'All right,' I say. 'You can tell a story, Terry.'

'Of course he can,' says Jill. 'I mean, what's the worst that could happen? It's not like the Story Police are going to come and arrest him for crimes against storytelling.'

'Story Police?' says Terry. 'There's no such thing. And, even if there were, they wouldn't arrest me, they'd probably give me an award for telling the greatest story ever told! Okay, here goes …'

In the beginning there was a ... um ... um ... um ... well ... now ... er ... ah ... well ... it's like this ... you see ... hmm ... uh-huh ... yeah ... I mean ... let's say ... right ... um ... um ... well ... now ... er ... ah ... well ... it's ... um ... er ... ah ... now ... er ... ah ... well ... you see ... hmm ... uh-huh ... yeah ... right ... right ... okay ... here goes ... here goes ... um ... um ... now ... er ... ah ... well ... you see ... hmm ... uh-huh ... yeah ... um ... er ... right ... um ... um ... um ... um ... um. Will you excuse me for a moment, readers? I'll be right back ...

'What's going on, Terry?' says Jill. 'Why has the story stopped?'

'Don't you mean, why hasn't it *started*?' I say.

'Well, that's the thing,' says Terry. 'I'm not sure *how* to start. Can you help me, Andy?'

'Why don't you try starting with *Once upon a time*,' I say. 'That's good for beginners.'

'Thanks, Pal!' says Terry. 'You're a real pal, Pal.'

'All right, just get on with it,' I say. 'The readers will be getting impatient.'

Okay, readers.
Here goes.
Once upon a time there
was a ... dot!

And the
dot was
all alone ...

●

but then
along came
another
dot ...

●

so then
there
were
TWO
dots!

●   ●

And then along came some more dots and soon there were LOTS OF DOTS!

23

LOTS AND LOTS
OF DOTS!

25

LOTS AND LOTS AND LOTS OF DOTS!

'Wow!' I say. 'Action-packed—or should I say *dot*-packed?'

'Shh, Andy,' says Jill. 'Give him a chance. I *like* dots!'

'But there's no *story*!' I say. 'He's just filling up the pages with *dots*.'

'I know,' says Jill, 'but it's strangely compelling. I can't wait to see what's going to happen next.'

And then, one day,
some of the dots
started joining up ...
and turning into lines!

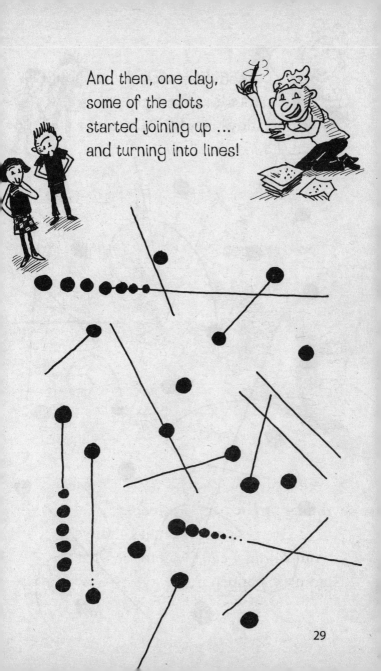

And then some of the lines started curving and bending ...

and joining up to make simple shapes!

And then those simple shapes started joining up and becoming more complicated shapes, like this ...

and this ...

and even this!

But the trouble was the dots and lines and shapes just kept multiplying ...

Maybe!

and multiplying ...

until they all exploded—

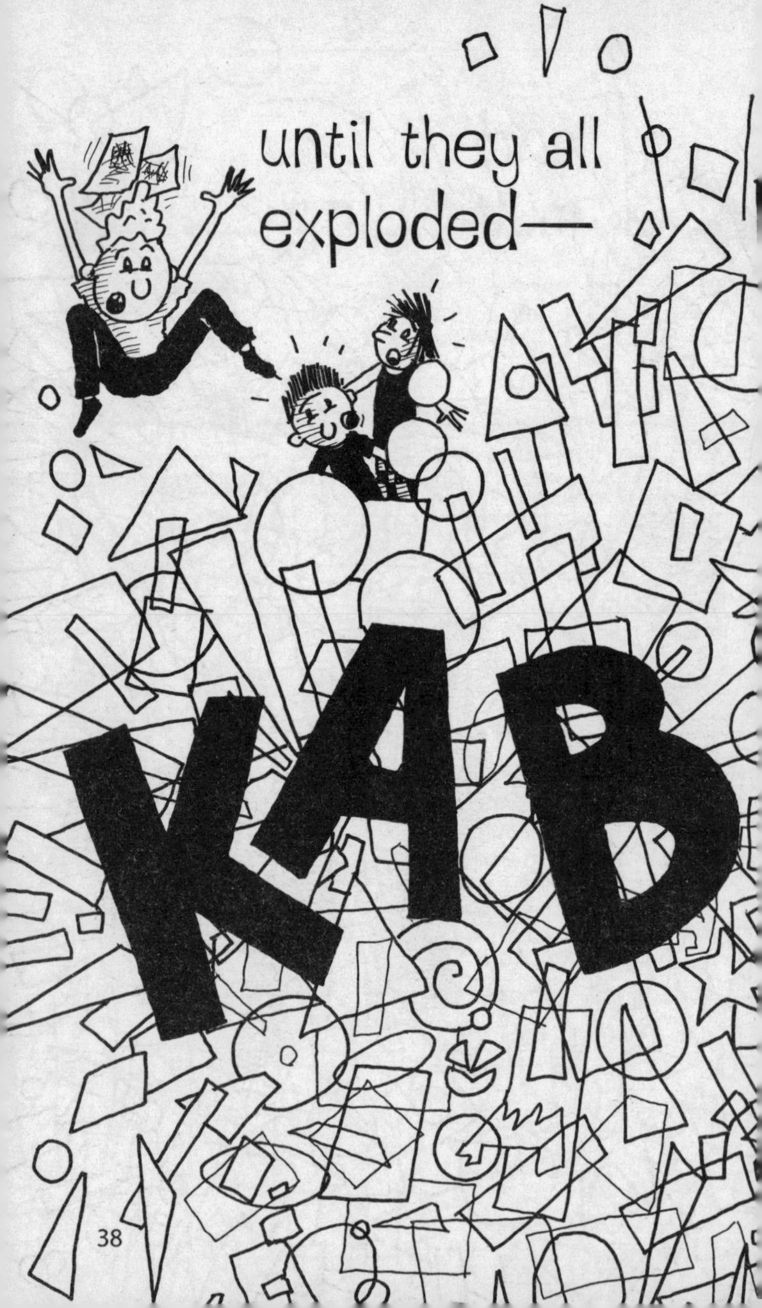

And after that
things weren't quite
the same ...

41

'Terry,' says Jill, 'what's happened to the story?'

'Well, after the explosion, the shapes started turning into all sorts of weird and crazy *new* shapes, sort of like what's happening to us right now.'

'Oh no!' I say, looking down at my body. 'What have you done?'

'I haven't *done* anything,' says Terry.
'You already were a collection of shapes
that joined together to form the shape of
a human being! You're still *you*, just in
a different shape—well, *lots* of different
shapes.'

'Well I don't like it!' I say. 'I knew
I should never have let you narrate!'

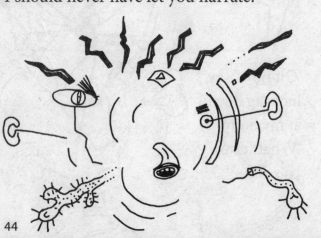

'Don't be too hard on him, Andy,' says Jill. 'The story isn't over yet. What happens next, Terry?'

'Well … um … er … ah … um … um,' says Terry, 'I don't know.'

'Well, that's just great!' I say.

Jill turns to me. 'What do *you* think should happen, Andy?'

'How should I know?' I say. 'It's *Terry's* dumb dot story, not *mine*. I've got no idea what happens next.'

'Gee,' says Terry, 'narrating is definitely *not* as easy as it looks. I should never have started a story that I didn't know how to finish.'

'I've got it!' says Jill. 'Why don't we call Professor Stupido? He's the world's greatest un-inventor. He could come and un-invent Terry's story!'

'Great idea, Jill,' I say, 'but Professor Stupido doesn't exist any more. We tricked him into un-inventing himself, remember?'

'Of course!' says Jill. 'I completely forgot. Why don't we get your Once-upon-a-time writing and drawing machine to finish the story? I bet that would know how to fix it!'

'Maybe,' I say, 'but we don't have it any more—the Birthday Card Bandits stole it and blew it up.'

'Oh yeah …' says Jill, 'that's right. Well, what about I call my animals? Perhaps they will be able to help.'

'I hate to break it to you, Jill,' I say, 'but the same thing that is happening to us is happening to them too. Look!'

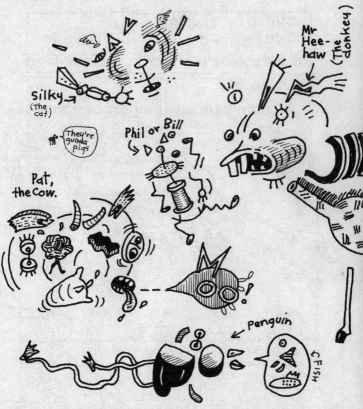

'Oh, no!' says Jill. 'My poor animals! This is like a bad dream—a *really* bad dream!'

'That's it, Jill!' I say. '*It's a dream!*'

'What?' says Jill.

'The key to ending this story,' I say. 'It's not the *best* way to end a story, but sometimes—if you're really stuck—it's the only thing you can do, and this *is* an emergency.'

I clear my throat and start narrating as fast as I can.

And then, suddenly, we all woke up and realised it was all just a DREAM— a really DUMB dream!

'You did it!' says Jill. 'Our bodies are back
to normal!'

'Yes,' I say, 'but I couldn't have done it
without you. You gave me the idea.'

'And you couldn't have done it without
me, either!' says Terry. 'It was my dots
that started it.'

'Yes, but it was *my* ending that finished
it and saved us all.'

'Actually, I'm not so sure about that,'
says Jill.

'Why not?' I say.

'Look!' she says, pointing to the
ground below. 'The Story Police are here.
They *are* real!'

'I know!' I say. 'I *told* you!'

'Yikes!' says Terry.

'Open up!' calls a loud voice from below. 'It's the Story Police here. We've had reports of a dumb dot story with a terrible *it-was-all-just-a-dream* ending coming from this treehouse and you are our chief suspects. There is no use resisting. We have your tree surrounded!'

'What do we do now?' says Terry.

'Open the door and let them in,' says Jill. 'I'm sure they'll understand if you just explain what happened.'

'No,' I say. 'That's not going to work. This isn't the *normal* police. This is the *Story* Police—they are really strict. We have to come up with a different ending … or else!'

'Any ideas?' says Terry.

'Yes,' I say. '*RUN!*'

and around ...

and around.

We run high.

We run low.

We run fast.

We run slow.

We go and we go and we go and we go.

59

'STOP!' says Jill, puffing. 'All this running isn't solving anything. It's not an ending—it's just *more action*.'

'Well, do you have any better ideas?' I say.

'No,' says Jill, sighing. 'I guess we'll just have to keep on running.'

'I think I might have an idea,' says Terry. 'How about this?'

 But just when it looked like all hope was lost, along came another dot.

'Oh, no,' I groan. 'Not more dots!'

'Give him a chance,' whispers Jill. 'It's our last hope.'

And the dot
got bigger ...

and
bigger ...

and
bigger ...

and the Story
Police all fell in ...

THE END!

Available in all good bookshops now!

YOU READ

OUT NOW!

PUZZLES TO SOLVE!

PICTURES TO DRAW . . .

GAMES TO PLAY!

THE TREEHOUSE FUN BOOK

JILL GRIFFITHS
ANDY GRIFFITHS
and TERRY DENTON

PACKED FULL OF ACTIVITIES BASED ON THE BESTSELLING TREEHOUSE SERIES

COMING SOON!

 FULL OF FUN!

THE TREEHOUSE FUN BOOK 2

JILL GRIFFITHS
ANDY GRIFFITHS
AND TERRY DENTON

FULL OF ACTIVITIES BASED ON THE BESTSELLING SERIES

If you have enjoyed this story,
turn the page for an extract from
another book you might like . . .

CHRiS O'Dowd
& NiCK V. MURPHY

MOONE BOY

THE NOTION POTION

ILLUSTRATED BY
WALTER GiAMPAGLIA/
CARTOON SALOON

MARTIN MOONE IS APPROACHING A MOMENTOUS MILESTONE . . .

. . . the end of primary school – and he's determined to get his face up on the Winners Wall before he leaves. Entering the invention convention with his motley crew of substandard scientists might be his only hope.

But coming up with amazing inventions is harder than Martin thought – so when his imaginary friend, Sean, suggests they get their hands on some Notion Potion, a mythical brain-boosting beverage, Martin leaps at the chance. But first he has to find his dream team of inventors . . .

TEAM MARTIN

So I was feeling a little groggy as I sat at
the back of the classroom listening to Mr
Jackson drone on. But Martin was wide
awake, eagerly putting his plan into motion.
And as their teacher handed out results of
a class test about what they did on their
science trip, the determined boy took note of
which students did best.

'Next up – Declan Mannion,' called Mr
Jackson from the front of the room.

As Declan went up to retrieve his results,
there were snickers from the rest of the
class. This did not usually go too well.

'What's the damage, Jermaine?' Declan
asked.

His teacher frowned at him, handing him
back the test.

Alan	D+
Other Alan	Had chicken pox so did not attend.
Trevor	B
Paul	Cat ate homework.
Marco	D-
Conor Bonner	E+
Jonner Bonner	E+ – Accused of cheating from a failing student. His brother confirmed allegation.
JohnJoe	C+
Dicky	Caught chicken pox from other Alan.

'F minus. We may as well get married, Declan – looks like we'll be spending the rest of our lives together in this classroom.'

There was a chuckle from the room. This soon died when Declan turned around and glared.

'No thanks, Jermaine. I'm never getting married again, but cheers for the offer.'

Declan walked off, leaving his teacher a little confused. Martin wrote down the latest poor result in his copybook.

'It's pretty slim pickings here, buddy,' I whispered.

'Yeah, when did kids get so dumb?'

'Trevor's got the best score so far.'

'He always does fairly well in tests. And don't his new glasses make him look particularly clever?'

'And so grown up,' I agreed.

'I should probably include him in the team – he loves being part of stuff.'

'Ah, yeah. It'll really make his day.'

The boy nodded, happy to be doing Trevor a huge favour.

'Trev . . .' Martin called, in a hushed but excited tone. 'Wanna be in a super-secret science team?'

'Yeah, whatever,' Trevor replied, barely looking up.

'Cool. Love the new glasses, by the way.'

'Thanks – they're my auntie's. Dad sat on mine.'

Martin turned back to me and I gave him an encouraging look. 'OK, so there's you. And there's Trevor. We're halfway there.'

But as Martin looked around the room, his

confidence drained from his already pale face. Was there anyone else with the Right Stuff to be on Team Martin . . . ?

During break-time, we were cornered by an irate Padraic behind the bike sheds. He'd heard about Martin's plan and was shocked not to be automatically included.

'But you've got to have *me* in the group,' Padraic insisted. 'What kind of party doesn't invite the P-Dog?'

'Like I said before, Padraic, it's not a party.'

'Not without me it's not.'

'I'll tell you what, P, why don't you use this opportunity to sell yourself to me?'

'How much? I'll not take less than a fiver.'

'No, I mean, tell me what you'd bring to Team Martin.'

'Well,' Padraic said. 'A better flippin' name for a start.'

'C'mon, P!'

'OK, OK. Well . . . I'm punctual.'

'I can't argue with that; you're a wonderful timekeeper.'

'I always carry a spare sandwich in my pocket,' added Padraic, pulling out a soggy sarnie from his trousers.

'Noted,' Martin noted.

'I'm good with animals.'

'Not sure how that'll help, but OK.'

'I'm excellent at maths.'

'That one is *not* true.'

'Nope, that one was a lie – I'll admit to that.'

'I dunno, Padraic. I really need the best of the best!'

'I put the A in team!' Padraic exclaimed, holding up his science results.

'Did you get an A in the test?' Martin asked, surprised.

'No, I got a C minus.'

'Well, there's no C in team, Padraic.'

'There's a C in cream. Can I be in some cream?'

'I want to win this thing, P, and I need every team member to bring something special.'

'OK, well, what you'll get from me is total loyalty. One hundred and ten per cent. Loyalty, plus the aforementioned spare sandwich.'

Martin considered his friend's plea.

'P-Dog – you know I can't say no to a sandwich. You're in!'

'In what?' came a voice behind us.

We turned to find Declan Mannion staring at us, with a cigar in his mouth. He was certainly not part of the plan.

'In, eh . . .' Martin tried to think quickly of something. 'In . . . school. I was just telling Padraic that he's in school. He was saying that this was a hospital, and I was assuring him that he's not having surgery today. Because he's in school.'

'Good save, buddy,' I lied.

'In what?' Declan repeated, this time looking at Padraic.

'We're all in a big party!' Padraic replied excitedly.

'It's not a flippin' party!' Martin hissed.

Declan noticed the entry form in Martin's hand and snatched it from his feeble grasp.

'What the flip is an Invention Convention?' he demanded.

'Oh, it's just some boring classwork-based nonsense. It's certainly not the kind of thing you'd be—'

'The winners get gold medals?' Declan noted, still reading the entry form. 'Grand, I'm in too.'

'What? But . . . I don't think you'll enjoy it, Dec—'

'I need gold. I don't trust paper money any more. All my operations are moving to gold.'

Martin looked to me. I shrugged. I've always liked Declan. He's the kind of guy that's good to know. In prison.

'Cool,' Martin lied. 'I'll let you know the details when I—'

But Declan had already walked off. He was in.

'*Now* it's a party!' Padraic added, before skipping off to the toilets.

Martin considered the newly formed team. He seemed less than impressed with what he'd just created.

'Sean, I bet those kids from St Whimmion's are as sharp as a Wonkey's front teeth. What have *we* got?'

I looked out at Padraic skipping happily away with a party in his step, Trevor poorly bouncing a basketball in his auntie's reading glasses, and Declan 'Can't-Stop-Failing-Sixth-Class' Mannion playing blackjack on a beer keg.

'It's not just about brains, Martin. Finding the right mix is the key to a successful team,' I told him confidently.

'I don't know, Sean . . .'

'Look at the A Team*. They've got a wily** old con man – for us, that's Declan. They've got the handsome charmer with a twinkle in his eye – that's Trevor.'

'Yeah,' Martin agreed. 'Those new glasses do make his dull eyes sparkle.'

'They've got the tough guy who's afraid of aeroplanes.'

'I did once see Padraic duck under a table when he saw someone making a paper jet,' Martin agreed.

'And lastly, they've got the crazy loon.' As I pointed at Martin, he seemed unimpressed by his status in the group.

'The crazy loon?'

'The wild card,' I assured him. 'The man of mystery who always surprises the enemy.'

'Well, I do surprise myself many times

*THE A TEAM – an underground crime-fighting force. Their mysterious endeavours were compromised when a documentary was made about them and broadcast on television throughout the 1980s and 1990s. They were then easily found and arrested by two policemen who watched the show.

**WILY – shrewd, astute and especially deceitful. Originally named after a gentleman named Willy, who was as canny as a fox, but a terrible speller.

daily,' he agreed. 'You're right, Sean. We can do this!'

'We sure can, kiddo. All we need now is a better name.'

'Hmmm,' Martin thought. 'How about The A-Team?'

'I feel like that one's kinda taken, buddy.'

'The B-Team?'

'The B-Team? Hmmm. I like it! I like it a lot.'

'Agreed, Sean!' he cried. 'What sounds more like victory than The B-Team?!'

WORLD
**BOOK
DAY**

Hello

We hope you enjoyed this book.

Proudly brought to you by **WORLD BOOK DAY**,

the **BIGGEST CELEBRATION** of the **magic** and **fun** of **storytelling**.

We are the **bringer of books to readers** everywhere

and a **charity** on a **MISSION**

to take you on a **READING JOURNEY**.

EXPLORE
new worlds
(and bookshops!)

EXPAND
your
imagination

DISCOVER
some of the very
best authors and
illustrators with us.

A **LOVE OF READING** is one of life's greatest gifts.

And this book is **OUR gift to YOU**.

HAPPY READING.
HAPPY WORLD BOOK DAY!

WORLD BOOK DAY

SHARE A STORY

Discover and share stories from breakfast to bedtime.

THREE ways to continue **YOUR** reading adventure

1 VISIT YOUR LOCAL BOOKSHOP

Your go-to destination for awesome reading recommendations and events with your favourite authors and illustrators.

booksellers.org.uk/ bookshopsearch

2 JOIN YOUR LOCAL LIBRARY

Browse and borrow from a huge selection of books, get expert ideas of what to read next and take part in wonderful family reading activities – all for FREE!

findmylibrary.co.uk

3 GO ONLINE AT WORLDBOOKDAY.COM

Fun podcasts, activities, games, videos, downloads, competitions, new books galore and all the latest book news.

SPONSORED BY

NATIONAL BOOK tokens

Illustrations © Jim Field

Celebrate stories. Love reading.